THE PRIZE FOR KINDNESS

THE PRIZE FOR KINDNESS

Okoli I. Victor

authorHOUSE®

AuthorHouse™
1663 Liberty Drive
Bloomington, IN 47403
www.authorhouse.com
Phone: 1-800-839-8640

First published by AuthorHouse   01/19/2012

ISBN: 978-1-4685-3156-5 (sc)
ISBN: 978-1-4685-3155-8 (hc)
ISBN: 978-1-4685-3154-1 (ebk)

Library of Congress Control Number: 2011963139

Printed in the United States of America

Any people depicted in stock imagery provided by Thinkstock are models, and such images are being used for illustrative purposes only.
Certain stock imagery © Thinkstock.

This book is printed on acid-free paper.

DEDICATION

I wish to dedicate this book to the Almighty God for His mercies and kindness on me. Also for His divine inspiration and vision that led to the birth and conclusion of this book. I say thank You Lord.

I also want to appreciate my parents, Ogbuefi & Mrs. George Okoli,my families and friends for believing in me.

Lastly,I also want to remember some people I missed that have gone to be with the Lord in Heaven-

Miss Frances Asuelimen;

Master Livinus Kanu (Dede);

Dr.Tony Okafor.

May their gentle souls continue to rest in peace, amen.

The Prize For Kindness
(Children Story)

This is the story of a young boy, Obinna Kingdom Okafor. He is 15 years old and lives with his widowed mother and little sister Ada, who is 10yrs old. They live in the town of Ughelli in Delta State, south-south Nigeria. Where he attends an all boys secondary school while his sister Ada, is in primary five. They relocated to Ughelli from the oil city of Warri after the death of their father. While Ada attends the primary school close to the little house they share with their mother, Obinna preferred an all boys secondary school rather far from home.

Obinna would run all the way to and from school everyday because his mother will not give him money for transportation from the little she makes from her petty trade at the main market. Obinna never asked his mother for transport money to school because he chose to attend a school that is far from home and he also enjoys the long distance race everyday.

One day as Obinna runs into the school compound in his usual manner, sweating all over. He was halted at the school gate by the games master, Mr. Umukoro.

What is always chasing you each morning on your way to school? The games master asked him standing in his way. Nothing sir, Obinna replied looking exhausted. What do you mean by nothing? The games master queried further. Then why do you always run into the school premises at such speed every other day? My house is far from here so I always run to school so that I will not be late. Obinna managed to reply, still panting heavily.

And you also run back home after closing so that you will not be late too? The games master asked again this time mockingly. I decided to stop you today because I have been observing you for some time now, the games master added. No sir, I run back home to pick up my little sister from her school and to also help my mother at the market. So you mean you do this exercise everyday? The games master asked again. Yes sir, Obinna replied clinching to his school bag, still sweating. Then why can't your parents provide transport money for you everyday? At least to protect you from other risks, like hit and run vehicles. Obinna raised his head to meet Mr. Umukoro's eyes; My father is dead and my mother is just a petty trader at the main market . . . Obinna was still talking when Mr. Umukoro interrupted him. That's alright, now go join the other students on the parade ground, it will soon be time for the morning assembly. Obinna thanked the games master and ran off.

Obinna Sat Down Watching Some Of His Class Mates Play Football On The School Field.

The time was 11:25am on a bright sunny day and the students were already out on break. The boys were involved in one sporting activity or the other. Some were busy with volleyball; others with basketball as Obinna sat down under a mango tree watching some boys play football on the school pitch. He was holding a book in his left hand but his attention was in the football game. The weather was clear and dry during mid day, conducive for sport so Obinna's friends took advantage of it to try out their soccer skills. One of the boys played the ball towards Obinna by mistake; Obinna, please play back the ball to us. Chike the boy who had played the ball towards him, pleaded. Obinna quietly stood up from where he was sitting, picked up the ball with his right hand and threw it back at them without saying a word. When will you ever play football with us? Kunle, one of the boys on the field asked, laughing. Obinna looked at him and answered; never. Why? Musa asked with his arms folded across his chest. I don't know why, Obinna replied as he goes back to sit down under the mango tree still holding the book in his left hand.

The Games Master Summons Obinna To His Office

Good afternoon sir Obinna greeted the games master as he enters the averagely furnished staff room. Good afternoon Obinna replied the games master, sitting relaxed in his chair. You sent for me sir, Obinna said calmly. Yes, come in and sit down here. Mr. Umukoro pointed at an empty chair directly in front of him across his office table. Obinna went and sat down quietly on the chair facing the games master in the empty room.

I have been watching you for some time now, the games master said as he stared straight at Obinna while adjusting his seat. You don't participate in any sports activity with the other boys non mix up freely with them either. You are always on your own, most times reading. Why? Obinna hesitated for a while before answering. My father was a very rich business man when he was alive, Obinna started. He made sure the family didn't lack anything no matter what it is. My mother was not doing anything then because my father would not allow her. My father extended his kindness to friends and other family members and everybody was happy. Then suddenly he fell sick and died. His friends turned their back on my mother, my little sister and I. His family accused my mother of killing their brother and threw us out of our home and seized everything my father had worked for, including houses and other properties. At this point, Obinna started to sob as he tries to control his emotions. Its okay, the games master tries to console him. I am very sorry about your father. Thank you sir Obinna replied as he continued his story.

My mother's elder brother who lives here had to relocate us from Warri and also helped my mother start her petty trade business at the market, here. One day my mother woke me up in the middle of the night and talked to me about all these pains we have passed through in the hands of my father's family and friends. I was so pained that I made her a promise, that I will take my studies seriously so I could take good care of my little sister and her when she is old. I know she did not take me seriously because to her I am a small boy. Do you sincerely wish to keep that promise? The games master interrupted suddenly. Obinna looked at him for a while then nodded his head gently. Then I will assist you to keep that promise, the games master said. How? Obinna asked inquisitively. Participate in this years' Great friends club endurance race and keep your promise alive; the games master added quickly. I have never heard of that sir, Obinna replied in a panic tone, looking calm. That is because you are new here, the games master retorted. Anyway, it is an annual sports competition organized by the Great friends club of this district for all the secondary schools here. It is strictly for sss2 and sss3 students. They will all compete for a chance to win a trophy for their school and also qualify for a university scholarship, courtesy of the club. I understand sir but I am . . . not good at sports, Obinna managed to say. I don't believe you, because you have not tried does not mean you can't. The games master replied, this time sounding a bit harsh. I don't understand sir; Obinna said looking confused. I must tell you one thing today young man; never undermine your abilities and potentials if you wish to keep your promise to your mother. Obinna looked at the games master with the corner of his eyes without saying a word. The games master stood up from his chair and walked gently towards the door and then stopped, backing Obinna and said. Always be ready to try out new things at all times, that is the best way to challenge yourself. Well, that is by the way. I am going to register you in the endurance race because I believe you can do it judging from how you run to and from school, daily. You should report for practice with the rest of the boys tomorrow. Obinna stood up quietly from his chair and walked to where the games master was standing, facing him he said. I can not participate except my mother approves of it; Obinna said in a very low tone. The games master looked down at him, placed his right palm on his left shoulder and replied; if that is the case, then I will go with you after school today to see your mother. Then he asked Obinna to go back to his class.

The Games Master Met Obinna's Mother.

Obinna and Mr. Umukoro the games master were both sitting on the same chair, at Obinna's mothers' stall at the market. Mrs. Okafor Obinna's mother is carrying Ada on her laps as she sat facing Mr. Umukoro. Are you sure my son has not caused any trouble in school? She asked again for the third time. No madam, he has not caused any trouble at school or anywhere; Mr. Umukoro answered, facing her and smiling. Okay, if you say so then I will believe you. Thank you madam, Mr. Umukoro replied still smiling. I need him to participate in a sport competition that I know he would do well in but he said I should first get your permission before he could compete. Mr. Umukoro concluded. Okay teacher . . . what you are trying to say is that; you want me to allow Obinna, my son, to represent his school in the competition. Mrs. Okafor asked, pointing at Obinna who is sitting beside the games master facing his mother. Yes madam, replied the games master flashing his teeth. What type of sport is that? Is it football? Mrs. Okafor asked at once. No madam, Mr. Umukoro answered as he tries to answer her questions. It is not football . . . this is a long distance race that is organized by the Great friends club annually, for secondary schools within this district. Ha! I thought it is Atlanta . . . Mrs. Okafor said, now laughing broadly. You are very funny madam. Mr. Umukoro replied as he tries to explain better. Atlanta is just the venue that hosted the Olympics back in 1996 where Nigeria won the gold medal for the football event. Atlanta is not a competition. This is a track event . . . I mean sprint; Mr. Umukoro went on. He can also go as far as to represent Nigeria in the Olympics if only you will allow him start now. Your boy can run, I know this . . . he only need your permission to do exploit. It is okay teacher; Mrs. Okafor interrupts. Reserve all these grammar for your students, she said laughing as Mr. Umukoro adjusted his tie in pride. I will allow him do the sport but I don't want him to get injured or fail in his school work; she concluded. That is where I come in, the games master said. I will guide him through training and I believe he will do well both in the competition and in class work. I thank you sir for believing in my son; Mrs. Okafor said as she goes down on her knees to thank the games master properly. No madam, the games master responded; you don't have to do that as he held up Obinna's mother back to her seat, smiling warmly. My interest is that he wins in his category and gets the scholarship to go to the university for free. My God will help him and also bless you too; Obinna's mother said pointing to the clouds with her right fore finger. Amen! replied the games master and Obinna at the same time.

Obinna Gets Some Motherly Advice

That evening after dinner Obinna's mother called him to sit by her. My son, she started. Since the death of your father and everything we went through in the hands of your father's family, we have been on our own. You have being an obedient son that is why I am allowing you to join in this competition. I don't have much to say but you should not allow success get into your head if you wish to succeed in life. My son, she continues. It pays a lot to do well and be kind to people in times of need no matter what is at stake. Obinna, did you hear me? She asked calmly. Yes mummy, I will not let you down; Obinna replied as they both retired for the night.

Obinna Joins The Other Boys For Practice

Mr. Umukoro gathered the students he had selected to compete for the only slot to represent their school to the school field. They were all dressed in white vest, a shot and a pair of white tennis shoe as recommended by the games master. Obinna managed to find his way to the front row, looking smart in his sport wears. Good morning students Mr. Umukoro said as soon as he stood firmly on a wooden table facing the participating students on the field. We all know why we are all gathered here today. Yes sir! The students shouted at once like they were soldiers on parade. Mr. Umukoro cleared his throat and continued. That is very good but let me just go through the details once more. We are all here to prepare and select the student who will represent our great school at the annual Great friends club endurance race as it is popularly known. All the secondary schools in this district will provide one representative each from amongst their senior classes and he or she will compete with the students of other schools in a long distance race at the township stadium in male and female categories. Mr. Umukoro continued as his voice echoed in the morning wind. As we all know, the winner of this competition will be given a scholarship to the university by the Great friends club of this district so we must all prepare very well this time around because we have never won this competition before, but I strongly believe that this is our year. I am going to split you into groups for the heats and only the winners of each heat round will qualify for the final selection. The student that wins the final selection will represent our great school at the competition. Now let the practice begin; he concluded his speech feeling happy with himself as the students clapped and cheered in admiration.

Obinna Qualifies For
The Final Selection

Beyond the expectations of most of the old students, Obinna made it through his group and qualified for the final selection. Mr. Umukoro asked the ten students that had qualified for the final selection to line up in front of him. He once again climbed the wooden table to address them. I am very glad that we have gotten the best of the best amongst us that will compete for a chance to represent our great school. You all have done very well he added, including those that have been eliminated. I am particularly impressed by the determination exhibited by some of you especially the newest student amongst us; Obinna Okafor. The final heat to select the best student amongst the ten finalists will hold tomorrow. So, you all should go home and prepare your minds for tomorrow. Yes sir! The students answered at once and went back to their various classes.

Some Of The Finalists Quarrels' With Obinna

The next day at the school field some of the finalists were practicing individually as they all await the arrival of the games master. Obinna was at one side of the field with Festus, one of his few friends as they quietly helped each other out in physical exercises. Obinna, do you know you are the biggest liar I have ever known? Maxwell one of the finalists said as Obinna looked up, surprised. What lies did he tell you? Onajite, an sss three pupil and the representative of the school at the previous years' competition asked Starring at Maxwell curiously. He told me yesterday that . . . this is the first sport competition he was ever involved in. Maxwell replied. Yes and that is the truth, Obinna said in defense. You see? Maxwell fumed as he stands to his feet. How can you get to the final of your very first sport competition? Can that ever be possible? He asked starring straight at Obinna. I can't see anything strange in that. Festus defended Obinna. Everything is strange about it because he is lying. Francis another sss three pupil took side with Maxwell. That is nonsense; you can perform well in your first sports competition, it all depends on your level of determination. Kenneth joined the argument. The argument became intense with all the ten finalists fully involved that they didn't notice Mr. Umukoro walk up to them. What is the argument all about? The games master asked as soon as he moves closer to the group. Why are you all talking at the same time? He asked again in his usual hash tone. Good morning sir! They all greeted at once. We are not arguing sir, Obinna managed to say . . . Then why were you boys shouting? Mr. Umukoro continued before Obinna could finish. Sir, we were only discussing how we are going to support our representative to win the competition, whoever he is. Onajite managed to find the right words. Well . . . that is wonderful. Mr. Umukoro said smiling sheepishly as he asked the boys to get ready for the final selection.

Obinna's School Gets A Surprise Representative

Mr. Umukoro informed the ten finalists that there must be a winner at the end of the final heat amongst them all and that who ever that person is, he would expect the rest of them to give him their full support. He went on to urge them to rally round the school representative to ensure that their school wins this years' competition for the very first time. At the end of the instructions he asked; do you understand? Yes sir! The boys echoed at the same time.

He then asked them to file out in a single line on the tracks and take a deep breath. At this point a large spectator made up of mainly students and some teachers have formed outside the tracks. The school principal was also watching the final heat from his office window up-stairs.

On your mark runners; Mr. Umukoro shouted at the top of his voice as the boy's struggles for comfortable space on the tracks. Set . . . and go. The boys took off like a herd of buffaloos at the sight of a lion. Kenneth led the pack followed by Festus and then Onajite who is still considered the favorite. Obinna maintained his tactics of coming from behind all the time as he tries to keep pace with the pack. He ran with a calculated precision, without allowing the pack in front to catch up with him from behind, knowing that will disqualify him. By the time Mr. Umukoro sounded the bell for the final lap Onajite was leading the pack with an appreciable gap while Obinna was now fifth in line. Obinna then increased his pace as soon as he heard the bell. He swept through the rest of the students in front of him like the harmattan wind. And before you knew it he was directly behind Onajite who tried all he could to maintain his lead as the spectators cheered with excitement. Onajite looked back from time to time to see Obinna's position as he ran while they both head for the finish line. Now it is clear that the race was between Onajite and Obinna as they were far off from the rest. The more Onajite tries to increase the gap between him and Obinna the more Obinna closes in on him. The race continued this way even as the finish line was in sight now. Obinna snatched the lead from Onajite with a clear body distance as he ran across the finish line to the excitement and surprise of the entire school. Obinna, Obinna! rented the air as some of the boys lifted him shoulder high while the entire school clapped in admiration including the school principal, clearly seen from his office window. Mr. Umukoro beamed with smile as he watched Obinna lifted shoulder high by other students and he was happy that he convinced him to join in the competition.

Obinna Informs His Mother About His Sellection

At the close of school Obinna ran home as fast as he could even though other students still wanted to jubilate with him over his qualification for the annual competition. He ran across the roads and streets leading to Ada's school like he never did before, smiling with excitement. He quickly took Ada from her school and headed for their mother's shop at the market to break the good news to his mother. Mummy, mummy!! He shouted from a distance as soon as he saw his mother. What is it Obinna? Why are you shouting like that? Mrs. Okafor asked placing her right palm on her chest as she looked disturbed. I am sorry mummy but I won the race, he said with excitement written all over him. Oh my God! You mean you have gotten the scholarship? She exclaimed! No! Replied Obinna. Then what race did you win my son? She asked again as her neighbors at the market watched in amusement. I have been selected to represent my school at the main competition next weekend, at the township stadium. It is only when I win next weekend that I can be given the scholarship. Okay, now I understand; His mother said calmly. So in your school you are the only person that will go for the competition next weekend. She added as she sat down with Ada on her laps. Yes mummy. Obinna replied happily. My son I am very happy for you but we can talk about it later at home. Go get your tray pan now and let me arrange those plantains for you, Mrs. Okafor said as she brings down a pack of ripe plantain from a table beside her.

Obinna Got Support From An Unexpected Person

On the day before the big competition being on a Friday, the school principal sent for Obinna through the games master. Obinna enters the beautiful office in the company of Mr. Umukoro. He greeted the principal who was sitting in his chair behind the office table as he admires the office with his eyes. Make yourself comfortable my young man, the principal said in his usual bold voice as Obinna sat down on one of the chairs in front of the principal's table. I only called you here to assure you of my support and that of your teachers. You should be brave as you carry this great responsibility on you tomorrow. Be rest assured that the entire school are behind you and do not hesitate to make any request from me through your games teacher should you need anything that will help you win this competition. At the end of the principal's speech Mr. Umukoro and Obinna both thanked the principal for his support and assured him of victory. Obinna, you now go back to your class . . . Mr. Umukoro instructed him as they both descended the step leading to the principal's office. As soon as Obinna turns to leave he heard his name from behind. He turned and saw Onajite standing some meters away from him. Obinna walked towards him not knowing what to expect. Onajite stretched out his hand for a hand shake as soon as they were close and Obinna took his hand in total surprise as they shook hands warmly and smiled at each other. I support you my brother, Onajite said to Obinna as their hands were still locked together. Thank you Onajite, Obinna replied feeling very happy as they both walked away still holding hands.

The 'D' Day

On the day of the competition Obinna woke up early, did all his house work and started getting ready for the journey to the township stadium. How do you intend to get to the stadium? You know it's far from here. Obinna's mother asked him after he has had his breakfast. Don't worry, I will run. Obinna replied, looking smartly dressed in his school uniform. No, I don't want you to be sweating heavily by the time you get there; the mother said. I will give you transport money that will take you there and bring you back early enough so you could come help me hawk those yams I bought yesterday.

She added as she prepares for the market. Thank you but I thought you are coming with me? Obinna asked looking a bit worried. No my son, I can not come with you because today is Saturday and I have to be at the market. But don't worry the Lord is with you, you will be fine. His mother said as she packs her bags.

Obinna joined a bus at the bus stop going to the township stadium. The journey took some time because the driver was always stopping every now and then to drop and pick up passengers who are standing along the road. The occupants of the bus were mainly elderly men and women who were either going to work or to the market. Obinna was excited watching the trees and buildings pass them by as he looked out through the bus window. Obinna did not allow anything distract him from watching the trees and houses go by in great speed as he placed his school bag on his laps. Not even the regular screams from the conductor as he calls for passengers disturbed him, he continues to stare at the buildings and tree as soon as the bus goes into motion after every stop made by the driver. Is there any stadium in this bus? That is the conductor's way of asking if any of his passengers would be coming down at the stadium gate as the bus heads towards the direction of the stadium. Yes! A woman sitting behind

Obinna shouted. I will come down at the stadium gate conductor. On hearing those words; 'stadium gate', Obinna jolted from his seat and shouted at once. Yes, yes!! I will stop here, please stop. Where do you want to stop small boy? An old man sitting beside Obinna asked him. I am going to the stadium, sir; Obinna replied looking uncomfortable. The stadium is still a pole away, the conductor only asked now so he would know if anybody will stop there; the old man informed Obinna. Where is the person who wants to stop here? The conductor asked. He will come down in front of the stadium gate and not here, the old man explained to the conductor. Then while did he ask us to stop here? The angry conductor quarried. He is only a small boy, forgive him. The old man pleaded; smiling at Obinna.

When the bus finally stopped in front of the stadium Obinna thanked the old man and alighted from the bus including some other passengers. He stood for a while admiring the structure with his school bag dangling from his right hand as people walked past him in and out of the stadium. He has never been to a stadium before so he imagined how the inside would look like as he took his first step towards the entrance gate.

Obinna Met His School Mates At The Right Time

The stadium is very big with the tracks neatly demarcated with white paints. Some men and women dressed in white T-shirts, trousers and skirts were standing in groups discussing while others were inspecting the tracks. At one end of the stadium were colorful canopies with white chairs under them for important dignitaries. Students of the various competing schools who had come to cheer their representatives were scattered everywhere. Some of the students were sitting down in the stands while others were busy moving in, out and around the stadium ground. Obinna has never seen such a huge number of persons in a single place before so he moved gently that he did not step on somebody. Watch your path, a strange voice cautioned beside him. He muttered sorry even before seeing who it was. You have stained my sander; a boy who is bigger and taller than him said from behind. I am very sorry, I didn't see you coming. Obinna pleaded looking terrified. The tall boy seized Obinna by the collar of his shirt. You will wash my sander for me now, he instructed. Please forgive me, I have no water. Obinna begged politely looking terrified. Let him go now, a third voice commanded from behind them. Obinna turned around and saw Onajite and other of his school mates that had come in his defense. And who are you people? The tall boy asked? Trying to scare them all. We are his school mates and he is representing our school here; Onajite answered for the group. And if you don't let him go now we will all beat you up together; he added. Obinna freed himself gently from the tall boy's grip and stepped backward a bit. The tall boy looked at Obinna and chuckled; this small boy, your school representative? He asked mockingly. With these tiny legs of he's I have nothing to worry about because I am also representing my school; he added. Size has nothing to do here, he is the best in our school and we trust him. Festus retorted. Soon, we shall see how well you trust him. The tall boy said, laughing as he walks away.

Onajite turned to Obinna; where have you been? Mr. Umukoro has been worried so he asked us to go search for you. Where . . . where is he? Obinna stammered. Come this way; Onajite led the way as they all disappeared into the crowd.

Obinna Met Mr Umukoro
At The Stadium

Obinna where have you being? Mr. Umukoro asked in a hurry. We have being looking all over for you; he added before Obinna could even answer the first question. Dress up and come with me at once, they are accrediting runners over there; he pointed towards a group of officials sitting in front of a table. He led Obinna by the hand towards the officials. Mr. Umukoro and Obinna stayed in line with other runners and their games masters who were also awaiting accreditation. Is this your runner? A female official asked Mr. Umukoro as soon as they got to the front of the table. Yes; Mr. Umukoro answered, smiling. He should be about the youngest runner I have seen today, the official said. Big surprises come in small packages. Mr. Umukoro joked. Well, you are certainly correct; I wish the both of you success. The official added as she hands Mr. Umukoro Obinna's accreditation card.

Obinna Joins Other
Runners On The Tracks

Don't allow anybody's size scare you Obinna, you are a good runner in your own right. Go out there . . . believe in God and in yourself and do all of us proud; Mr. Umukoro advised Obinna. Thank you sir, Obinna replied. Now go join the other runners on the track, Mr. Umukoro said smiling. Obinna nodded his head and ran towards the tracks.

Runners take your positions on the tracks, the umpire who is wearing white all through and holding a dummy gun in his right hand instructed the runners. According to the size of this stadium you are expected to complete a six lap's endurance race to become the winner of this competition. I mean, the person who comes first at the end of the sixth lap becomes the winner of the male event. Now listen to the instructions; the umpire continued. Do not run until you hear the sound of this gun, he instructed putting up the gun with his right hand for the boys to see. If you run before the sound of this gun you will be disqualified so watch and listen carefully; the umpire added. These instructions made Obinna scared as he starts to sweat on the forehead.

Runners on your marks, the umpire shouted aloud again. Get set . . . he continued. At this point the entire stadium fell silent and Obinna's heart beat increased. Then suddenly . . .

'Gboooo', the umpire's gun went off and all the runners took off apart from Obinna. The umpire's instructions and the cheering crowd had increased his tension that he did not hear the sound of the dummy gun. He stood there on the tracks confused until he managed to hear Mr. Umukoro's voice . . . Obinna don't stand there, run, runnnn! Mr. Umukoro shouted at the top of his voice. And on hearing the voice of his games master Obinna took off like a wounded lion towards the other runners in front.

Obinna Does Something Strange On The Tracks

Obinna quickly joined the pack of other runners from behind with lightening speed. He looked through the pack of anxious runners in front of him to gauge the distance between him and the person in the first position. After the first lap, gaps started to form between the runners as they struggle for positions. That was when Obinna realized he needs to edge closer to the front. Gently and precisely Obinna pushed closer to the front, wrangling in and out of the pack of runners, almost unnoticed. Obinna pushed to the fifth position just before the end of the second lap, then the bell sounded for the third round. At the sound of the bell Obinna tries to edge his way pass the runner in the forth position but he kept shielding him with his frame. After two attempts without success, Obinna decided to step away from the pack a bit into the outside tracks. He made use of his new found space to increase his momentum. Cruising freely past the forth and third runners swiftly as the spectators begin to follow his small size with their eyes. Obinna's brilliant performance made the entire stadium stand on their feet so they can see him clearly. Everybody focused on Obinna as he finally placed himself in second position by the fifth lap and begins to aim for the first position.

Half way into the sixth and final lap Obinna edged closer with every stride towards the first position as Mr. Umukoro kept following his every move with his eyes. The runner in first position suddenly looked back to see those behind him and he quickly recognized Obinna as soon as their eyes met. He was the tall boy who had asked Obinna to wash his sander earlier in the day. On recognizing him Obinna doubled his speed. The tall boy also tries to maintain his position but the more he runs the more Obinna gets closer and closer with ease. On seeing Obinna's improved effort his school mates started chanting his name to encourage him; Obinna,

Obinna, Obinna!!! As his name echoes in the afternoon heat inside the stadium, Obinna's effort improves as he caught up and past the tall boy, placing himself in first position and continues to extend the gap between himself and the rest of the group. The finish line tape was raised and Obinna heads towards it as his school mates kept chanting his name endlessly; Obinna, Obinna, Obinna! to the admiration of other spectators. Then suddenly the tall boy who is now in second position behind Obinna fell heavily to the ground as he screamed at the top of his voice. Oh my God! I am dead . . . my left ankle is broken! My left ankle is . . . please somebody help me and he crashes heavily to the ground and cried out loud. Obinna who is now some few meters away from the finish line turned to look at the tall boy who is now lying in pains on the ground with nobody interested in his injury as the entire stadium was focused on Obinna. Nobody bordered to attend to the injured boy as the other runners jumped over him and continued running while the officials were also urging Obinna to finish the race just like the other spectators. The crowd were urging Obinna to finish the race and claim his trophy but to the surprise of the entire stadium, Obinna turned and ran back towards the tall boy on the ground. He held him up and supported him off the tracks towards the officials before joining the race

again. At this point some of the officials ran towards them
and took the tall boy from Obinna. What do you think you
are doing? Those were the hash words from Mr. Umukoro as
he screamed at Obinna from where he was standing with the
other students; Go back and continue the race! he continued
to shout . . . looking physically stressed with anger. By the
time Obinna got back on the tracks the boy formally in
third position was now in front of him and very close to
the finish line. Obinna charged towards him like a wounded
lion but it was far too late as the boy crossed the finish line
before Obinna could even get close to him. Obinna fell on
his knees and bowed his head in disbelieve, it was like the
entire stadium was coming down on him. He could not
believe he had just lost a race that was as good as he's. He
had just disappointed his school principal, his games master,
his friends, school mates, himself, his mother and dashed
his dream of a scholarship. All these thoughts past in a flash
before his very eyes as he knelt there and starred at the floor.
With tears rolling down his cheeks he watched as the winner
of the race was lifted shoulder high by his school mates.
Nobody came to him not even Mr. Umukoro. He managed
to pick himself up and walked quietly through the crowd to
collect his bag from Mr. Umukoro who is looking every inch
very angry. Mr. Umukoro is standing close to the stands with

Obinna's school bag in his left hand and looking very moody. Some of Obinna's school mates were standing close to him as they were all sweating profussly from the intense heat of the afternoon sun. You just lost a race that was clearly yours' out of shell foolishness. Those were the words of Mr. Umukoro as he drops the bag on the ground and walks away angrily. His school mates and friends stepped away from him one after the other without saying a word to him. After a while Obinna was standing all alone, he picked up his school bag and walked towards the stadium gate with his head bowed in shame as other students looked at him in disbelieve. He got into a bus heading home and sat quietly in one of the back seats and this time, he was not gazing through the window to watch the trees and buildings go by.

Obinna got down from the bus when he got home and for the first time he walked home quietly along the street rather than run home happily.

Obinna's Mother Met Him At Home, Sick

Obinna's mother got worried about him when she did not see him at the market. When she couldn't get anybody to ask after Obinna from she decided to close and go home on time. She left the market with Ada strapped on her back and hurried home, trying very hard to hide her fears as she walked pass people she knew on the way. She was surprised to meet Obinna at home sleeping inside the bedroom instead of coming to help her hawk yams at the market. Obinna was still putting on his sports cloths and this made his mother more angry. Obinna! Obinna! she called out his name, shaking him by the hand to wake him up. Obinna woke up after a while, feeling very weak. Did I not ask you to come hawk those yams I bought yesterday? You have never disobeyed me before; what is wrong with you today? She asked again, this time in a hash tone. I don't know what is wrong with me but it feels like I have fever; Obinna managed to say without sitting up. You have fever? When did it start? His mother asked. Now stand up and let's go to the medicine store across the street for some drugs. Obinna stepped down from the bed, led the way and his mother followed with Ada as they all left the bedroom.

Obinna's Mother Consoled Him

Later that evening after Obinna had taken his drugs after dinner, his mother asked him about the out come of the competition at the stadium and Obinna narrated the entire event that took place at the stadium to her. At the end of his story, his mother laughed instead of saying sorry and this bordered Obinna greatly because he expected some sympathy from his mother. I thought you should tell me sorry rather than laugh at me, Obinna queried. She stopped laughing and cleared her throat. Don't ever expect anybody to have pity on you over something you did or did not do; his mother cautioned. So you mean you are not angry with me? Obinna asked looking surprised. Why should I be? His mother asked in reply. To me, you did what you thought was right at that point giving the circumstances. Showing kindness to a fellow human, to me, is the greatest victory you could ever wish for. Mummy, Obinna interrupted. Yes? His mother answered, looking up from the work she was doing. I just want to remind you that I will not be getting the scholarship any more, Obinna said; sounding sober. I know my dear. The God that gave you the kind heart to abandon the race and assist the boy in pains will make another way for you. She assured him; placing her left arm across his lean shoulders. Thank you mummy. I feel a bit better now, Obinna said; sounding very bright. At least you understand my actions, he added. Don't worry; your friends will come back when they realize that who you are is different from what you are; his mother consoled. Obinna hugged his mother and said, thank you mummy again.

Obinna Got A Visitor At Home

Obinna stayed at home on Monday and Tuesday because he was still on drugs and also needed some rest. His mother also asked him to take the time to rest and not to border coming to help her at the market.

Obinna! Obinna! somebody called from across the compound. Yes? Who is that? I am coming. Obinna replied from inside the house as he walks towards the door to see who it was that called. He came outside and was surprised to see Mr. Umukoro standing in front of him. Mr. Umukoro was dressed in a white long sleeve shirt and a grey trouser and smiling at him. Good afternoon sir, Obinna greeted as he smiled back at his games master. Good afternoon Obinna; Mr. Umukoro replied warmly. I decided to come and know why you have skipped school for two days now. Mr. Umukoro said placing his left palm on Obinna's shoulder. Who showed you my house, sir? You have never been here before; Obinna asked. Your mother directed me. I went to see her at the market, Mr. Umukoro replied. So why have you not been coming to school Obinna? Mr. Umukoro quizzed. Obinna looked at him and replied; I have fever sir. Mr. Umukoro squatted in front of him held his hands and said. I understand what you are going through, you are not happy with the way I and your friends treated you the other day at the stadium. Its normal for you to feel bad, I beg you to forgive us and put the whole thing behind you now. Mr. Umukoro consoled him warmly. I shouldn't have walked out on you and for that, I say sorry. Mr. Umukoro added. I am also sorry sir, for letting you and the school down. I did . . . what I thought was right at that time. Obinna apologized. Mr. Umukoro looked at him and said; I understand better now, the boy was in serious pains and your good heart led you to assist him not minding what is at stake. That's okay, I believe there is a reward for every kindness shown to a fellow man. Mr. Umukoro encouraged him to come back to school soon. Thank you very much sir; Obinna thanked his games master and they embraced each other.

Obinna Back At School

Obinna attended school the next day after the visit at home by Mr. Umukoro. The sky was bright on that Wednesday morning as students walked through the school gate in small groups. Obinna walked in quietly as if he is new to the environment. For the first time, he did not run into the school compound like he use to do. He also tried as much as possible to avoid eye contacts with any of the other students as they gazed at him closely. He was just approaching the assembly ground when suddenly he heard somebody call out his name; Obinna! He turned around and saw Musa, Kunle, Chike and Onajite running towards him. Why did you miss school for two days Obinna? Musa asked, hitting him slightly on the chest as the four of them caught up with him. I . . . I had fever; he managed to reply. Oh sorry. We could have come to visit you at home if we knew your house; Chike said. But I can see you are alright now, Kunle added smiling. Yes, Obinna replied (nodding his head). I feel much better now, thanks for your concerns. Obinna said, feeling relaxed. I hope it was not because of the event at the stadium that you fell ill? Onajite who have been keeping mute joked; grabbing Obinna playfully from behind. No . . . not at all, Obinna stammered. I am sure it is, Onajite continued. But don't worry . . . you will get over it soon, he added amidst laughter. They all joined in the laughter as they walked to their different classes.

Obinna Got A Letter

It was on a Friday morning and the students and teachers were all gathered at the assembly ground for the morning formalities. After the parade and the recitation of the national anthem and the usual announcements, the principal stepped forward to address the students. Facing the students he said, good morning all of you. Good morning sir! Replied the students. We have once again come to the end of another wonderful week; the principal continued. I say wonderful due to some of the events that led us into the week. Notable amongst them was the drama some of us witnessed at the township stadium last Saturday, he said smiling. Which is not common with him. Obinna's heart beat increased at the mention of the township stadium. As we all know, our school has always wished for the day we will lift the Great friends club endurance race trophy and scholarship. And this time we came very close but like I mentioned earlier, a drama happened between our representative, Obinna Okafor and one other student from another school. And that drama cost us the race. Well, I don't know about you but if you ask me. I will tell you it was a case of the biblical Good Samaritan or we should call it; the good Nigerian? Everybody except Obinna laughed at the principal's joke because he wasn't sure of him yet. The principal smiled a bit and continued. No doubt, Obinna Okafor did our school proud out there at the stadium. Only that he did not get the trophy for us and the scholarship for himself. All the same, I thank God because He alone knows why what happened, happened. At this juncture I would like to introduce to us this gentle man in our midst this morning. He is here to share something with us. He then pointed at the middle aged man that has being standing beside him and ushered him to come forward. The man was neatly dressed in black suit over a stripe blue shirt and a black pair of shoes. The man stepped forward and introduced himself. My name is Mike Mudiaga. I am the PRO. of the GREAT FRIENDS club of this district and the organizers of the annual endurance race. (This attracted some rounds of applause from the students including Obinna who is a bit relaxed now) Some of you may be quite angry that your school did not win the race because your representative chose to be kind over a clear victory. That is by the way for now; he added. The GREAT FRIENDS club of this district have asked me to inform you all that your school have been invited to a grand reception in honor of your representative, Obinna Kingdom Okafor. (Everybody turned towards Obinna) He should please step forward if he is here with us; the man in the black suit said. Obinna please come to the front now; the principal echoed in his usual high tone voice. Obinna gently moved to the front from behind, looking scared as everybody tries to catch a glimpse of him. Congratulations, the PRO said as Obinna got to him. This is the invitation letter for your school to the grand reception. It is to honor your courage of kindness even in the middle of a competition. They both shook hands and Obinna handed the letter to the principal and walked back to join his class on the assembly and everybody applauded as the principal put up the white envelope containing the invitation letter, for all to see.

Obinna Had The Last Laugh

The venue of the grand reception was packed full with members of the GREAT FRIENDS club, invitees and other dignitaries. Everybody was looking neatly dressed in their best out-fits and the time was 10:10am when Obinna walked in with his mother and Ada. Good morning madam. Mr. Umukoro greeted Obinna's mother as soon as he saw them walk into the nicely decorated hall. Good morning teacher. She replied. Smiling happily. I am so glad you were able to make it madam; Mr. Umukoro said. Knowing fully well that Saturday is very important in the life of every market woman, Mr. Umukoro continued. You are very correct but what can I do? especially after I got your message through my son. Thank you for the respect madam. Mr. Umukoro added. Where can we sit down now? The whole place is almost filled up; Obinna's mother asked Mr. Umukoro. Well, I don't know the sitting arrangement yet but you can come and sit down over here for the time being. Mr. Umukoro led them to some empty seats in front of the hall. Obinna was dressed in a fitted light grey suit with a waist coat and a sparkling white shirt to match, over a pair of black shoes. His mother wore wrapper and a beautiful blouse while Ada wore a simple gown and looking happy also. There are so many notable persons at the high table including Mr. Umukoro and the principal. Musa, Kunle, Chike, Onajite and few of Obinna's school mates sat directly behind him on the second row while others were at different points in the large hall. Obinna and his friends also noticed that various schools were invited including the school of the boy who eventually won the race. Obinna was also able to recognize the wounded tall boy as he waived at him from a wheel chair across the hall. They were still busy looking round the hall when suddenly the public address systems came alive. Hello!the voice of the MC (master of ceremony) echoed through the loud speakers. Please get seated because I am about to hand over the microphone to the chairman of the occasion to say the opening prayer before we commence. He handed the microphone to a very huge man sitting in the middle of the high table facing the hall. The huge man who is dressed in a well tailored native attire, stood up and cleared his throat into the microphone. Which caused the big speakers to quake. I am Mr. God's day Ajoromi; the huge man said. I am also the president of the GREAT FRIENDS club of this district and I welcome you all to this grand reception of the greatest sports man I have ever seen in my life. How else can you describe the actions of last Saturday at the township stadium? That day I saw love in its real form. I saw kindness in the midst of a battle and perceived victory. It was amazing. Without wasting much of your time, I would like us all to bow our heads in silence for sixty seconds as we commit this occasion into the Almighty hands of God our father. At the end of the sixty seconds, Mr. Ajoromi shouted a big Amen! And everybody sat down as he handed back the microphone to the MC. Thank you very much Mr. Chairman, the MC acknowledged. Without wasting much of your time, I would want to call on the star celebrant; Master Obinna Kingdom Okafor and his family to please come over to the high table. The entire hall erupted in applause as Obinna, his mother and Ada walked up to their new seats. I will also call on master Obinna to come to the front of the stage and tell us what actually inspired him to do what he did last Saturday at the stadium. The entire hall cheered and clapped as Obinna made his way to the front of the hall. Took the microphone from the MC in his tiny palm as he looked shy. With the microphone in his little right hand he said; I . . . I decided to help the other runner because my mother will always want me to show love and kindness to fellow humans no matter what is at stake. When he injured his leg and cried out for help I felt very sorry for him. The entire hall erupted in loud cheers and clapping before he could conclude. Wonderful! What a big heart of kindness for a small boy, the chairman said with the microphone in his hand. At this point, neatly packed foods and drinks were served to the occupants of the hall by some smartly dressed ladies. I have never seen anything like this before even in the international scene; the chairman continued. For this show of kindness the GREAT FRIENDS club international have therefore decided to honor master Obinna Kingdom Okafor with an international scholarship award.That will enable him attend any university to any level in his chosen career, in any country of his choice.Those announcements from Mr. Ajoromi threw everybody in the hall into jubilation especially members of Obinna's school.The father of the tall injured boy also gave Obinna a cheque for the sum of N300,000.00 (three hundred thousand naira); as a compensation for losing the race as a result of his kindness towards his only son. Obinna was also appointed as an ambassador of love to the GREAT FRIENDS club international and an award plaque was presented to him. Obinna's mother was very happy as she shed tears of joy. She also thanked Mr.Umukoro for believing in her son and selecting him for the competition. The event ended with everybody struggling to snap photographs with Obinna and his family and everybody went home happy.

THE END.